THE OTHER WIFE

A TWISTED TALE

RUCHIRA KHANNA

ISBN 979-888521429-2

"There are some people who live in a dream world, and there are some who face reality; and then there are those who turn one into the other."

– Douglas H. Everett

Other Books by the Author

viewauthor.at/RuchiraKhanna

• v •

- Bowled, but NOT OUT
- Choices: A Novel
- The Adventures of Alex and Angelo
- Voyagers into the Unknown
- Breathing Two Worlds
- R.S.V.P: A Novel
- Doppelganger-A Short Story
- Through His Eyes: A Short Story
- How to Weave a Theme into your Story –*Non- Fiction*

"You don't get it, Dimple. You've changed so much that I don't even know you sometimes," Rishi said in an agitated voice and turned his back to me.

My tears felt hot and prickly as they touched my cheeks. "Just breathe, Dimple. Just breathe!" I muttered to myself.

I continued contemplating the day's events and realized that I found my husband and the circumstances were to blame, so I was baffled as to why he condemned me.

Then I tried to play the whole scenario with the old me he had fallen in love with, but I couldn't find her within. I twisted and turned in the tiny space I had courtesy my better half, who had taken most of the bed.

No such luck!

The back-and-forth search made my tears stop, but the drama continued within. Even though my eyes were shut, my mind was in a turmoil. The scene looked like a Presidential debate where both the candidates—my mind and the circumstances—were speaking simultaneously, not giving my intellect any reason. Amidst the chaos, I didn't realize when my mind hit the snooze button.

***

"Hi!"

I turned around and, with a frown, greeted the girl back.

"Aren't you, Dimple?" she said.

"Umm, yes, I am. How do you know me? Who are you?"

"I am Pearl," she said with a broad smile that showed off her even teeth just like mine. Although hers sparkled like in a toothpaste advertisement.

"Okay, but who *are* you?" I asked, quite irritated at this rude interruption as if she had just pinched me hard.

"I am Rishi's wife." Her manner was cool, the way a cucumber mask gives coolness when peeled off the face.

"Rishi who?" I inquired with a frown, a little confused about where she was leading with this.

"Rishi Malhotra. Yes, you heard it right. I am *your* Rishi's wife."

I shook my head with annoyance and tried hard to concentrate on what this lady was trying to tell me. Just then, another lady nudged me. "Are you going to buy this?"

I looked at the scarf in my hand; it didn't attract me anymore. I shrugged and was quick to give the scarf to her. I had enough distractions and wanted to focus on Pearl, whose smile refused to leave her face and irritated the socks out of my shoes.

I didn't hesitate to drag her by the arm and pull her to a corner. "You are making no sense. I am Rishi Malhotra's wife. It's against the law to have two wives in Hindu culture." I said in a stern low-key voice.

"Oh! You needn't worry about the logistics." She became defensive. Then after a pause, she said, "Let's be friends." She extended her hand toward me.

"Friends? Why?" I shrieked as if I just saw a cockroach on her.

There was a toxic smell around me, and I was sure it was coming from my burning heart.

I was quick to place my hands over my bosom. *Oh my God! I'll die before confronting Rishi over this.* My nostrils flare up whenever I am angry, and that's when I realized the smell felt like that of rotten eggs. "Nah! Somebody must have farted next to me. This smell is worse than when I drive my car with my hand brake on. Now that's what you get when you talk to strangers in a packed mall," I muttered to myself as I wiped my forehead with force, as if trying hard to erase what fate had written for me: another wife.

"Treat me like your soul-sister. I'll make sure to pamper you and even help show you the way."

I frowned upon her comment and didn't hesitate to give my opinion. "Huh! How can my husband's second wife be my best friend?" I howled and didn't care if people passing by stopped to glance at me. After a brief pause, I inquired, "By the way, when did he marry you?" I quickly pulled out my phone to get answers from Rishi since his so-called second wife was making no sense at all.

She was quick to take away my phone and walked into a store.

I was taken aback at first, then quickly followed her. "Hey," I shouted, "give me back my phone."

"Look at this," she picked up a garment and pressed it against my bosom. She turned me around, so I was facing a mirror. "This blouse suits you so much."

I was in no mood for shopping. I wanted to throw that garment away, but Pearl held it tightly to my body.

"Just breathe," she commanded.

How does she know my code word for when I'm flustered? Has Rishi spilled out all my secrets to her? How dare he!

"Give me back my phone. I need to call Rishi and get some answers." I groaned.

She continued, "Doesn't this color make you look confident? So savvy and fearless."

The words confident and fearless echoed in my mind. I wanted these big fat adjective pills inside me to confront Rishi when I met him.

I looked at my reflection. I liked what I saw, but then I also saw Pearl in the mirror. I stared and pursed my lips, and with a quick, jerky movement, I pulled away from her.

"What happened? You don't like it?" she asked with raised eyebrows and wide eyes.

"Do you expect me to shop when I've got the news of my husband's second wife?" I scowled.

"But I'll help you find your way. I know you're lost."

"Huh!" I gave her a dirty look.

I pulled her out of the store, toward a bench and forcefully made her sit next to me. This time forces had become our unapologetic twin.

"I want to know who you are. How did you meet Rishi?"

She was playing with her fingers just as I did when nervous.

"Can you please give me my phone?" I pleaded. Then I rolled my eyes since that kind of language should be coming from her. After all, she is the 'other' wife.

She got up and started walking.

"I will call the cops!" I said out loud.

"Go ahead," Pearl said as she waved at me just like the queen would upon seeing her fans.

I hated her guts and wanted to strangle her. Her personality was nowhere likable, but I know why Rishi fell for her. I, too, used to be like this once upon a time. Was it that trip he went to, his so-called business meeting? He was without any cellular network at that remote place, and we were out of contact for those unlucky thirteen days. Sigh!

I was on pins and needles during that time. Although now I wonder why? My insecurities had built up during those days. I was as fragile as a loose tooth.

"Are you coming?" She called out to me.

Her words brought me out of my reverie, and I immediately got up as if a teacher had commanded me. I took quick steps to catch up.

Wait a minute! I am the first. She is second. Shouldn't she be following me?

I halted and shouted back at her, "I am not coming."

"Why?"

"Umm, I have to go to the restroom." Saying that I turned and looked around for a sign.

In no time, she was beside me and showing me the way.

I was puzzled but followed her anyway. When about to enter, I handed her my purse out of habit.

"Take it with you. I am nobody's server."

How rude! I carried my stuff with me.

While emptying my bladder, I realized that dialogue was familiar. A long time ago, I used to utter those lines to anyone who asked for favors. I was a working professional then and always thought I had touched the sky until I came down with a bump. Jeez! That bruise was still blue on my buttocks, but at the same time, I had given my heart to Rishi.

Speechless, I approached her, surprised to see she was waiting patiently for me.

"Let's eat," she announced.

"I can't be eating with a homewrecker!" I demanded, "I need my phone back."

"Sure. But don't you want answers?"

I was quick to nod.

"So, that can only be done while sitting. Right?"

Umm . . . okay."

"What's with the 'umms' all the time? Do you always take this long to decide everything in your life?" she snapped at me with a twisted smile.

I got annoyed at her frankness. *How dare she?* But as we walked toward the food court, I realized how picky I had become over the years. 'Never realized I had changed so much. I was not like this.'

Soon, she beckoned me from a table while I was still deciding what to eat.

"Life sure passed me by. Why do I take forever to make decisions about me, myself, and I?"

I slid into a chair across her.

I noticed people carrying shopping bags pass us by as they browsed the storefronts that announced sales. I had also visited the mall with the same intention—to shop for bargains. Alas! Life threw me a curveball with the name Pearl.

"So, tell me now. I need to know." I urged. Felt ashamed over my reaction and blushed hard over it.

"Jeez, look at your nails, your hair, your eyebrows. Do you ever take time for self-care?" Pearl inquired.

I hated her guts but still chose to clarify.

"Yes, I go to the gym every day. That's close to my house," I said with confidence, this time. "Nails and threading, I usually get done when I have errands to run and have the car to myself. As you may already know, we share a vehicle."

"Since you are here, do it today."

"Who are you to tell me what to do and what not to?" I burst out, my index finger pointing toward her eyes.

Surprisingly, she didn't blink even once and continued to wear a smile.

I do need to look my best before I confront Rishi.

Then after a pause, I added, "Umm, okay."

"Thank goodness," she said with raised eyebrows. "You do know that I'm looking out for you?"

'How I wish she would leave Rishi and me alone?' I muttered with the corners of my mouth turned down.

"What happened?"

After a brief pause, I said, "I wasn't always like this, just so you know." My eyes were moist as I let out a forceful breath. I stopped munching my food, and frowned as if recollecting my past, trying to find words. "All I know is that marriage changed my personality, and with Rishi backstabbing me with another wife, I feel betrayed." I poked my tongue against the inside of my cheek, closed my eyes, and lowered my head.

There was silence as we both continued to finish our food.

I looked up now and then, wanting to know more about her, but was scared that she'd point out my shortcomings, leaving me either embarrassed or confused.

She is a tough cookie.

While walking toward the salon, I checked her out. She was tip-top. Her accessories were not frippery, but she carried them with confidence.

I liked how she had styled her hair. She smelled good too. And the way she could steer the car was so smooth, unlike my driving skills that are always bumpy when I shift gears.

***

It's been over two hours since I'd met Pearl, and I have not yet been able to get any information about her. She's been scrutinizing me, and she even has my phone!

She is a control freak. It reminded me of somebody, though—me.

While I was getting myself pampered, I checked her out in the reflection of the mirror. She was sitting patiently. I was quite surprised by her stability and concentration. Unlike the rest of us, this lady chose to stare out the window and not at her phone. She seemed like a mannequin to me from afar. No emotions, no movement. Just playing with her fingers now and then. Very odd, indeed.

Once all prim and proper, I approached her, and she gave me a broad smile. "Now, that's more like it," she exclaimed, and the twinkle in her eyes was genuine.

I grinned and, like a schoolgirl, flipped and flopped out of the salon with her by my side.

"Oh! How I wish she were not Rishi's wife." I muttered with a groan, "Why has life thrown such a twister at me!"

"So, what else is on your agenda?" she inquired.

I stand still, place my hands over my hips, "My agenda is to know why did Rishi remarry? You refuse to give me my phone, and I'm getting very impatient, now." I refused to be polite, and she could sense my agitation.

"Alright, let's go to that cafe, and I'll tell you everything."

Now, the fact that I'll know everything made me very nervous. I realized my life would not be the same after she bares the truth. Rishi was my love, for whom I betrayed the trust of my parents. Little did I know he'd do the same thing. Karma is a bitch! I bit my lips and dragged my feet toward the cafe. When we sat down, I continued to be fidgety.

"So, tell me about yourself?" she asked.

"Huh?" My mouth fell open, and while my fingers were touching my parted lips, I gave her a dazed look.

I was furious and was quick to get up. "Listen, lady. It should be the other way around. I have no clue who you are, what you do, and how you found me." I was so loud that people in the cafe stared at me.

"So strange. She doesn't know her, yet she's having a drink with her?" I overheard a lady at the adjacent table, talking to her friend.

I blushed hard and stared at the tile flooring and the decorative flower pots around me.

Pearl was calm; she continued to sip her chai latte.

After a couple of silent minutes, she asked the same question again.

"What do you want to know about me?" I gave in.

"Your past, that has changed your present. You were quite upset about it."

"How do you know?" I squinted my eyes even as my lips started quivering. *Gosh! Rishi is such a tell-tale.*

She chose to wear a steady smile instead of answering.

After a few sips of my chai latte—yes, we both happened to enjoy the same drink—I said, "Rishi must have already told you about my past. What more do you want to know?"

"I only know something's changed in you, but I don't know the reason why," Pearl said.

I had a sly smile. *Huh! So, there is something that even Rishi could not tell about me.*

Then after a pause, I started my story.

"Ever since I got married, two nicknames surround me. One is FB and the other 24 DDD. You can add a cheating husband, now." My voice caught in my throat as a sob escaped me.

Blame Pearl for getting intimate with my life!

I looked at her with moist eyes, hoping to get some consolation, but instead, she was staring at my breasts.

When she noticed that I had caught her in the act, she said, "Well, I am just trying to figure out why the triple D. You have an almost flat bosom."

"Oh my God! You have such a dirty mind," I shrieked and didn't hesitate to keep my voice down.

What followed after that was obvious. I had many onlookers, and just like that, my eyes refused to shed any more tears.

I sat down with such a jerk that my chair bounced back, but I was quick to grab the table, so the front legs of the chair that were in the air were short of hitting the ground with a bang!

Drama queen, indeed.

"What makes you do such things? Were you always like this?"

"My city Kanpur was a loving and peaceful community until a young, dynamic, bank teller, Dimple Kapur, had the ambition of becoming a manager of that branch—"

"Hold that thought," exclaimed Pearl, and was quick to get a refill. Then she made herself comfortable, just like one would before the start of a movie. "Carry on."

***

I gave her a wicked smile, similar to that of Glinda from *The Wizard of Oz.* I realized I wanted to relive my past and hopefully have a better present than what I have right now, just like those time travel movies.

I started narrating my story to Pearl with a deep sigh, her eyes as curious as a five-year-old who has been offered a box of chocolates for the first time.

I started my narration again.

"Before I met Rishi, I was a young and ambitious lady whose only goal was to have a successful career. When Rishi came into my life, I was vulnerable and gullible, and he rescued me from all the negative spotlight. I fell head over heels in love with him and did not hesitate to run away with him after my parents objected to our alliance. The two happiest days of my life are, incidentally, the two worst days for my parents—one was when I got an acceptance letter from my employer, and the second was when I got decked up as a new bride.

"Numbers always fascinated me, and I got my undergraduate degree in economics. My parents and relatives thought I was a smart kid since I landed a job in a reputed firm. I was on cloud nine with constant praises from my family and became pompous and a snob. My success got to my head. My mom nicknamed my success as a virus that'll infect my whole body, but I didn't pay heed to her words. I was the first girl in our family to step out as a professional. I had to wear a uniform to work, the same kind of saree each day, but that didn't deter my confidence. My parents saw me change into an obnoxious, rude, and short-tempered person. The Bank of Scotland had high-class clients. I moved in sophisticated circles, drank coffee and tea in bone china cups, ate in a pantry full of fancy wrapped food, and worked in an air-conditioned cabin from 9 AM to 5 PM even though there were power outages in my city. All these comforts were so delightful that when the clock struck 5 PM, the thought of going home and being around ordinary people ticked me off.

"I was like a falcon flying high. My ego was as big as my shadow, but one day it came crashing under the big boots of my manager. My co-worker stole some money from the treasure box, and unfortunately, I was there at the wrong time. I was booked for fraud and was arrested. My parents came to my rescue. They believed in me, so they filed a case against my employer and hired a reputed lawyer.

"Mr. Batra, my lawyer, and his thick mustache were the talk of the town. He was the second-best in our city after Mr. D'Souza, who was my employer's lawyer. Rishi was Mr. Batra's assistant. He was a petite, frail guy in his early twenties. There were times when even Mr. Batra lost confidence in my case and would ask me upright, 'Tell me honestly, did you steal the money?'

"I would burst into tears and would not hesitate to cry loudly and, at times, even beat my chest over my fate. Yes, I was a drama queen even then.

"Mr. Batra would get hassled over my reaction and take a step back. I could see him sweating profusely, especially on his big nose that resembled a potato. The sweat beads could be seen vividly on it, just like snow on a mountain. My tone had sobered down, and so did my actions.

"My family was happy to have their affectionate, humble Dimple back. At night, my mom and grandmother would keep me warm with their embraces. During the day, Rishi would accompany me and whisper encouraging words in my ear. But his keen eyes and his thin lips were what always caught my attention. The court rulings used to be harsh, brutal where they threw my character in the sewage. Even our Kanpur sewage had better quality water than the abuse sprayed on my name. I would be heartbroken hearing all that. Mr. Batra would stand and argue with my opponent's lawyer while my ex-managers eyes scrutinized me. Meanwhile, Rishi would hold my hand and even squeeze it occasionally while muttering, 'Breathe, Dimple, breathe!'

"Those three months were as gruesome as a bear ruffling through a car for food. The bear would toss and turn the vehicle, even break the glass, to get hold of that food. The people in the court, the society, were just like that animal. I didn't hold back my tears. Rishi was the only one who dared come into my zone and comfort me until I stopped crying. He would lend his handkerchief to wipe my tears, and his gentle taps on my shoulder were enough to make me vent about life and this incident. With an occasional blow of my nose in the napkin, I would relieve myself. 'You can keep it,' he would say when I tried to return the piece of cloth to him.

"This episode of venting and crying helped me claim many of his handkerchiefs. I had started collecting them, washed and neatly piled in the corner of my cupboard. Finally, after three grueling months, the court announced I was as clean as a slate. I jumped with joy and didn't hesitate to hug Rishi in the court. My parents' reaction was also relieved, but my action in the court made them inquire about my feelings about Rishi. I was honest. My parents were shocked. Rishi was flattered that a 'famous' Kanpur girl had feelings for him.

"Yes, I had become famous since the local newspapers discussed my case. A journalist named Sikander had been following my story, and whenever I stepped out of the court, he used to click a picture of me. I was hesitant, shy, but he didn't care. The next morning, my partially covered face would appear on *The Kanpur Times*, and I would sniff and curse my fate. Today, after being declared innocent, I stepped out of the court with confidence and posed in front of Sikander. I gave a side view pose with a pout, and boy, this Kanpur girl set some high standards for my local sisters.

"Back home, while I was flying high due to the victory, my parents had a frown on their faces. I inquired, and my dad came to the point, 'What's going on with you and that lanky assistant of Batra Saheb?'

'I like him, Papa. He helped me during these three months of trial. He was by me during the court sessions.'

'He is an assistant; earns a meager salary. How will he support you?' was his reasoning.

'I have full confidence that he will be an even bigger lawyer than Mr. Batra.' My confidence was ardent.

The Universe listens... and I have proof.

"Rishi not only became more successful, but he also gained more weight than Mr. Batra! But those days, the argument kept going on in my household.

"Months rolled by. I chose to do my Masters as I was hesitant to go back to work even though they offered me a better pay-scale and position. But that scar of being called a thief by them had not yet healed. Rishi had moved to New Delhi. He was working for a reputed firm, and we were in touch via letters and texting. I enjoyed my audacious, carefree, flamboyant student life courtesy of my dad, who supported my frivolous expenses.

"One day, Rishi planned to visit me from Delhi. I was on pins and needles since he didn't give me any information on where I should meet him. When the doorbell rang, I opened the door, clueless as to who would be on the other side. It was my beau. I got nervous upon seeing him, so I quickly pushed him out and shut the door behind me.

'What are you doing here?' I asked, my eyes wide and my teeth clenched.

'It's high time we give a name to this relationship, Dimple. I've come to take blessings from your parents.'

Breathe, Dimple, breathe. Just then, the door opened. 'Who is it?' asked my dad.

'It's Rishi, Papa.' I gripped his wrist tightly and pulled him in. I noticed he had gained flesh around that once-slender wrist.

"Forcefully, I made him walk toward our living room, pushed him on the couch, and then sat next to him. My dad, in the meantime, shouted out to my mom. Like 'buy one get two free' offers, not only mom but my grandmother also walked out.

"All of us sat in the eleven-by-fifteen room. There was complete silence except for the fan circling round and round. Their glares made me uncomfortable, and I squeezed Rishi's hand. Rishi chose to take my hand and pat it gently. I liked his confidence and smiled at him. My dad deliberately made an attempt of clearing his throat. That action made me nervous. I was quick to take my hand away and went to sit on the other end of the couch.

'Hello, Mr. Kapur.' Rishi stood up and greeted my dad politely.

"He was dressed casually in jeans and a t-shirt. I could see those toned muscles underneath his clothes. Rishi had neatly combed his hair, and his spectacles gave him a mature look. His briefcase, somehow, got me confused.

Maybe he is here for a case. Dad gave him the silent treatment. However, my grandma inquired 'How have you been?' with a smile and a twinkle in her eyes.

"My grandma, whom I call daadi, seemed to be in favor of him. Hopefully, my parents will follow suit. I crossed my fingers. Mom was also seated next to my grandma. Just then, daadi instructed my mom to get tea and snacks. She, in turn, was quick to go inside and order Ramu kaka about it. Dad didn't sit. He gave dirty looks at Rishi and then at me. I was nervous and fiddled with my fingers.

"There was an eerie silence at first, but soon after, the tea arrived. Small talk began.

Dad chose to slurp his tea standing, while daadi kept inquiring about Rishi and his career.

My beau then opened his briefcase and took out some papers. He got up and handed them to my dad.

'I'll be able to support your daughter. See, this is my bank balance, and I have even bought a car, a Maruti 800. It's on loan now, but I plan to pay the installments soon.'

My Papa scanned the papers with raised eyebrows. 'I'm happy that you have advanced in your career,' he remarked. Then he sat down, facing Rishi. The papers were still in his hand.

"The rust-colored curtains that were once moving due to the light wind suddenly became stationary, as if anticipating and dreading his next move. Unlike a Maruti car with a regular engine, my heart was racing like one with a turbo engine. But the cozy room with bright colored sofa and glass decor seemed to cradle me as my dad continued to give Rishi more dirty looks.

'Any property?' Papa inquired as he placed those papers on the glass center table.

'Sir, I still live in a rented one-bedroom place, but as you can see my bank balance, I have the potential to own an apartment soon.'

I tried to scan those papers from the other end of the sofa. I could only see black ink. Damn! I wish I had worn my reading glasses.

'When you own one, you can come back and ask for her hand.' said my dad and walked out of the room.

'But Papa, I'll be very old by then,' came my abrupt response.

Dad paused for a bit, looked at my mom and hissed, and walked away.

'Then it's good that you didn't marry him,' said my mother as if that hiss was what my dad had intended to say.

Grandma was saddened at their reaction and walked out of the room.

"Rishi, with a pale face, was placing his papers in his briefcase. I held his hand and whispered into his ear to wait. Then I quickly walked to my room. I came back with the pile of cleaned and ironed handkerchiefs.

'Your property,' I said with a smile, hoping to cheer him up, but he simply kept them in his briefcase with a grunt.

I turned around and inspected my surroundings. Nobody was around, so I was quick to give a peck on his clean-shaven cheek.

He got excited by my action.

I was thrilled.

"To keep him in that state of mind, I whispered into his ear, 'Don't worry. We can elope and get married and will stay in that rented apartment of yours.' He blushed. I held his hand and squeezed it. He dropped the papers in excitement. I helped him pick them up, and our heads banged against each other.

'Ouch!' I said out loud, to which my mother came to the scene. Darn it! She escorted Rishi out of our home.

"I acted a scene out behind her back of running away and exchanging garlands. He nodded with a gentle smile, so my mom got curious.

She turned back to look at me and shrugged. 'Look at his audacity. I am pushing him out of the house, and he smiles.'

Little did she know the plan we were cooking. She shut the door on his face.

"A week went by. My parents refused to talk about him. But I continued to make plans for our secret marriage. My college friends helped me with the project while Rishi was game for any command from my end.

"Then that auspicious day came when all our plans and dreams became a reality. I had thought that eloping would be easy, but it took me two weeks of preparation before the final day arrived. "Planning and lots of patience are needed whether one chooses to elope or marry in front of the family. I went to college at the usual time but was picked up by Rishi on the way. We chose to get married in a court in an adjacent city, Lucknow. Being a lawyer, Rishi had planned everything out. My friends had gifted me a red dress, which I wore in the courtroom bathroom.

'Are you sure?' asked Rishi before I was about to sign the papers.

'Absolutely!' I said with a beaming smile.

"There was no guilt, and once we had exchanged the garlands and got the marriage certificate, I decided to go and meet my parents. Rishi agreed with me, but first, we chose to treat my friends who had helped us. We celebrated with a massive banquet in Lucknow, followed by lots of picture taking and laughter.

"In the evening, we drove back to my home. I was excited to present myself to my parents—the new me. Mrs. Rishi Malhotra.

"I made sure I looked like a newlywed in the proper traditional attire—with vermilion on my forehead, a gold mangal sutra adorning my neck, and bangles for both my wrists that jingled with every move—a gift from Rishi. I made sure I had the flower garland around my neck and the intricately embroidered red dupatta over my head. I was also aware that a bride ought to be shy and gentle, so I lowered my head and placed the red scarf over my face when I rang the doorbell.

My mother opened the door. Since the veil hid my face, she didn't recognize me. 'How can I help you?' she inquired.

"I looked up, and our eyes met. She looked aghast as her eyes went cold, hard, and her upper lip curled. I could tell she wanted to utter some curse words but couldn't find her voice.

I got terrified seeing that side of my mom, and my face turned pallid as if I had donated bottles of blood. With clammy hands and trembling lips, I tried to hold her, but she was quick to push me away.

"Tears started to roll down my cheeks, and Rishi was quick to hold my shoulders and pat them gently. Just then, mom lost her balance, but Rishi supported her. He was my knight in shining armor who came to her rescue, and

I was very proud of him at that moment.

"As she collapsed in his arms, I quickly dashed into the kitchen to get some water. My dad, who had recently arrived from work, heard the chaos and came out from his room. When he saw me in that attire, he was confused but even more confused to see my mom in Rishi's arms.

'What's going on here?' he yelled.

I ignored him and sprinkled some water on my mom's face, who had fainted.

Then my husband (ooh, felt so good to say that!) and I lay her gently on the floor while my dad grabbed a cushion from the couch and placed it under her head.

'What just happened here?' he asked while rubbing her hands and feet while I continued to sprinkle water on her face.

'She fainted,' I stammered.

'I can see that,' he said with scorn. 'And what are you wearing? Did you perform in a drama? And why is this boy here? Has he already bought a house?'

He asked so many questions that I didn't know where to start.

'Oh, God! What happened to her?' Out came my dear daadi, lamenting.

Since she couldn't bend, she stood over our heads and continued to bawl and instruct us.

That was a good distraction. I just couldn't handle another family member lying next to my mom.

'Don't move her. Let's call the doctor.' Those were some of my daadi's instructions that we all obeyed.

Dad was quick to call the doctor, and luckily, he was in the neighborhood. The luxury of being in a small city is that doctors make house calls.

He came in and examined her. In a few minutes, he was injecting something in her vein.

'Don't worry, Mr. Kapur. This medicine will help her.'

I was thankful at the handiness of him having such a shot in his briefcase.

While we waited for her to gain consciousness, daadi asked me to prepare tea for the doctor and even Rishi.

That's our Indian custom; we serve everyone. *Atithi Devo Bhav.*

Mom gained consciousness, and the first four words out of her mouth have become my nickname in my family since then.

'My 24-year-old Dimple turned out to be disrespectful and deceitful.' Aka 24 DDD.

Then the whole drama unfolded. My father and grandma also had things to say, but they weren't as harsh as 24 DDD.

"I was heartbroken upon hearing it all. I wanted to scream but could not speak. I tried to run into my room, but my limbs felt unsteady, and I felt dizzy. I tried to get up but plopped right back on the ground. I had tears in my eyes, but I held my breath, which made my stomach feel as hard as a rock.

"While my parents and grandma were busy accusing me, Rishi was noticing all this. He picked me up, and we walked out of the house.

I could still hear them curse me.

"The car journey back to his home in New Delhi was a silent one. I was shocked since I didn't expect them to react in such a way. I wanted time to go back so that I could be their obedient daughter again, but I was dozing off in no time. But the sharp honk of a truck on the freeway woke me up with a jerk, and I realized that I am the actual 24 DDD.

"I've been married to Rishi for two years now.Fortunately, my parents allowed me back into their home and their lives, but that nickname does not leave their tongue as if it's been permanently tattooed on my forehead.

"My mom's taunts, my dad siding with her, and my grandma continuously nodding are all I get when I visit them. These reactions make me want to rush out of that house within an hour.

Now, that negative vibe that I get from them needs an outlet, and Rishi is the victim. I take out all my pent-up anger on him. I lose my temper at a mere pinprick, so he has nicknamed me a Fuse Bulb, aka FB.

"Although now, on second thoughts, I feel I did him right given that he secretly married a second time. Alas! My life is revolving around these two nicknames in both of my homes."

I stopped narrating my life story and let out a deep long sigh. I placed my long brooding head on my hand, resting on the table.

But Pearl had no empathy. She gulped the last bit of her chai down and smacked her lips. I looked at her with piercing eyes, having second thoughts on why I had confided in her.

"So, how do you plan to get rid of these nicknames?" she asked.

"Forget the nicknames; I'm thinking of ways to get rid of his other wife first," I said out loud.

Some onlookers stopped and gave a cold stare.

But she did not react.

My ears turned red, and I dipped my chin down in embarrassment.

Then after a pause and a couple of swallows I said, "How can I get rid of the nickname? My parents are my life and blood. I will have to live with their acronym until I breathe my last. Although now that Rishi, the love of my life, has married another lady, I'll probably go and live with them."

"Wrong!" she shouted.

I was taken aback by her response.

"Let the old Dimple come back," she said with a stern look.

"The old Dimple has been gone for long," I said with a sigh.

"Stop this self-pity and these sighs."

Pearl was very determined, and I could see her jaw clench over it.

"But how?"

"What is done is done. The only reason your parents continue to use those acronyms is because of the backlash from society. Secretly, your parents must be happy at how Rishi has provided you with all the comforts. You have moved into a two-bedroom apartment that you own. So, don't punish yourself and continue to be in the dungeon." Pearl added, "Next time you visit them, put an end to it. Tell them all has ended well, and request them to stop using those names since it's hurting you and your relationship with your husband."

I was stunned by her support.

"You make it sound so simple," I said.

"They are your parents, after all," she added.

I liked Pearl's suggestion but was curious why she was helping me. After all, she is the other wife. What will she get out of it?

I contemplated it and couldn't find the answer. So, I asked her point-blank, "What's in it for you?"

"Huh?"

"You know if I follow your advice, then Rishi and I will live happily ever after, and you'll be out of the scene. So, why are you helping me?"

I had expected Pearl to be antsy, but she was as still as a rock. She had a smile on her face, and that got me very confused.

After a brief pause, she demanded, "Just do what I say, okay?" She got up from her seat.

I quickly got up and followed her as a kitten would her mom.

After a few steps, we reached the exit of the mall. Pearl stopped. She pulled out my phone from her bag and handed it back to me. "Alright then. It's settled. You get your husband and your life in order." She started walking out.

"Wait!" I called out.

She stopped with a frown.

"Can I give you a lift home? Where do you live?"

"In your heart!"

***

When the alarm clock blared in the morning, my eyes immediately opened wide. I tried to make sense of my surroundings.

I stared at the art piece that hung on the wall opposite my bed. Then I scanned around and saw the TV, some clothes lying on the single couch, and a man next to me.

"Oh, Dimple, could you please snooze the alarm?" came Rishi's request, that I was quick to adhere.

Then I frowned when I realized he was lying next to me. I raised my eyebrows upon seeing him. "What! Rishi is here. Then who is with Pearl?" I muttered and sat up on the bed.

I was quick to pat Rishi aggressively.

"What?" he demanded as he turned toward me with an agitated look. "Now, what did I do to fuse your bulb?"

"Where is Pearl?"

"Who is Pearl?" he inquired with squinted eyes.

"Don't counter question me, Rishi," I said with a stern voice, to which he sat up.

Seeing his confused look, I came to the point, "I know that you have a second wife, Rishi. I saw it all. I met her in the mall, and. . ." Suddenly, I was faltering as words escaped me.

"What nonsense! I can't take care of one wife, and I'll go and marry another one? That's ridiculous!" Rishi said as he threw his comforter off his body and reached out for his phone on the side table.

"Anyways, I have a plan to make our lives happy. You'll forget your other wife once all this is settled."

Rishi had a confused look as he looked up from his phone.

"Yes, Rishi, you are looking at Dimple 2.0," I said with pride as I got up from the bed. "Please book my bus ticket to Kanpur. I would like to visit my parents. I am going to tell them about my feelings and request them to stop calling me names. I'm sure if not my parents, at least my daadi will understand me. After all, I am her precious Pearl."

"Pearl?"

"Pearl! OMG. *I am Pearl.*"

I jumped upon Rishi after realizing that it was a dream; his phone went flying. Thankfully, it plopped on the bed.

"Rishi, I had a dream where I met your other wife, who was a part of me, and she tried to make sense of my life."

"Huh!"

"Oh my God!" Saying that, I burst out laughing as if somebody was tickling me hard.

He turned back to look at my face and got very confused while I continued in a loud decibel, "What a dream! I was terrified at first, but now it's an OMG moment."

Rishi was staring at me with his mouth wide open and a frown.

I feared that he'd judge me and label me with another acronym, but this dream was an eye-opener for me. It was as if my subconscious told me to live my life on my terms, just how I was before I got married to Rishi. I remember my father always lecturing me to break boundaries in life, but when I broke one, he sided with my mother even after umpteen apologies. Today, it's my turn to open his eyes and request him to let bygones be bygones.

Why was I living an insecure life? No wonder I am always confused and utter an 'umm' before making every decision. Why was I getting intimidated at everything that came my way?

Pearl acted as my guardian angel to bring that awareness within me. Although I was making an effort to change myself because of the competition between her and me, my heart still longs for Rishi. If I set my feet firmly on the ground, nothing can shake my confidence.

This dream was not merely pointing out my metaphysical problem but had a reversion of the mind into its abode, from the world of sensory operations.

"I don't get you, Dimple," Rishi said as he lit his cigarette and blew a puff of smoke. "Why would one have such a dream?"

I was in full explanation mode, so I started, "If a tiger attacks you in a dream, you wake up with sweat all over the body. You may even cry. This is possible, right?"

He agreed.

I went on, "You may fall from a dream tree and dream-break your legs, and you feel real pain. Sometimes, the legs start trembling even when you wake up. You start touching them to see what has happened to them. You take some time to realize that nothing happened, and then say, 'I was dreaming.'"

Rishi seemed convinced, but not for the fact that I could dream of his second wife. So, I continued, "Dreams, therefore, can have umpteen causes. Whatever the causes are, dreams in the individual are regarded as an effect of waking and are often judged due to impressions of waking, perception, and cognition. Your real personality, at least partially, comes out in the dream world. Dreams, therefore, are due to repressed desires."

"Wait a minute!" he interrupted me, "So, you are not happy, thus the dream of another wife?"

I shook my head in negation, but after a pause I nodded, which meant a yes.

"Every human being has an obsessive notion, and it's not just one but several such complexes that are inside them. If these notions are not fulfilled, it leads to frustration, which leads to disappointment. An individual then tends to suppress those desires within, which is a repressive activity. Repression and suppression are the mind's mechanisms to appear harmonious by putting on an appearance that is not real. When you suppress a desire, you become an artificial person. You are not what you are."

"Simpler terms, Dimple!" urged Rishi as he held his head over the jargon.

"After I eloped with you, I was attacked verbally by my mom, and my dad and grandma followed. The confidence that I had grown after my court case came crashing down as if an elephant had walked over me. All my desires came crumbling down. After that, all I wanted from them whenever I visited was respect. For years, I wanted to be called just Dimple by my parents. But that was nowhere in sight. So, I chose to put on a smile for you. While I was suppressing my desire to be loved by them, it affected my ability to make decisions since, deep inside, the after-effects of deciding on marrying you were gnawing at me. I eventually took it out on you and started losing my cool over your little shortcomings, for which you nicknamed me as a fused bulb."

There was silence.

I was in tears.

Rishi was quick to come and hug me affectionately. "I'm sorry for what you went through. The reason for your short temper never occurred to me."

"But aren't you glad the other wife came to my rescue? If these buried impulses had stayed like this for a long time, it could have led to some physical disease or even a divorce," I said with vigor.

"You're right. Let's settle this with your parents like adults."

"What! You want to come too?"

"Absolutely! We have to solve this issue with them. After all, you're my only wife." Rishi winked at me," The courts are closed this Saturday, so let's go this weekend."

***

I was eagerly waiting for Saturday as Rishi insisted upon coming with me to Kanpur. In the meantime, I was doing the prep talk in front of the mirror while writing it down.

"Mummy, Papa, I have come here to apologize sincerely, and I am hoping that you forgive me so that we can all end this drama and have a happily ever after."

Oh! Is there ever a happily ever after? I don't think so. I was confused by my earlier line, so I crumpled the paper and chose to write again.

"Hello Mummy, Papa, I am going into depression, and only you can help me now. Please forgive me so that we can start our lives on a happy note?"

"Depression? Really? Nah!"

I crumpled the paper again.

"See what you have done to my life, Mummy, Papa? I cringe at making every decision ever since I've got married. I've lost confidence in myself. All this can change if you forgive me, please."

Not too fond of the tone here. I crumpled the paper again.

That day I was busy with the write-up on how to approach them. I never realized it would be so tough until now. Later that evening, when Rishi arrived from work, he was dismayed to see piles of papers.

"What's all this?" he inquired in a severe tone.

"Oh, Rishi. I am so nervous. I can't even write a proper apology dialogue for my parents." I bawled.

He was quick to hug me. "Go with what your heart desires."

"That's the problem. My heart shuts down in fear when I see my parents' faces as my mind shouts back at me on how I've ruined their reputation in the society, and their knitted brows and angry tone become justifiable." Then after a deep pause I added, "That's why I thought it would be better to have it written so I can avoid overthinking."

"Well, whatever you think right, go for it." Rishi said as he washed up after his long day at work.

The days rolled by, and soon I woke up to a Saturday morning. The chilly, crisp night gave way to sun-warmed earth, and the flowers opened their buds and released their divine scents. It created an uplifting scenario, given my day's schedule.

"Come on, wake up, sleepyhead. We should start early to avoid the traffic. We don't want to spend the whole morning on the roads. I would rather spend that time with my parents." I cooed as I pulled the drapes and opened the window to allow sunshine into our room.

I smiled when I heard birds chirping and the dogs barking.

"Oh, Dimple, let me sleep."

"See, that's why I wanted to go by myself, but you kept insisting. And now you prefer to sleep." I couldn't control my tears and sunk into the bed with my hands over my eyes.

Whoever said tears could make any husband spring into action is right. Rishi was quick to push his comforter on the side and was sitting next to me.

In an hour, we were on the freeway.

I had packed a bag which had our nightwear, just in case things get sorted out. I was hoping to spend the night there, with my parents.

A girl can only hope!

I had chosen a red blouse to pair with my jeans while Rishi wore a white shirt and trousers. While my husband was driving, my fingers kept fidgeting on their own.

Rishi observed that and tried to distract my attention by inquiring, "What's with the dark-colored shirt in this hot weather?"

"I always used to wear red color when going for exams, and this is not a different day."

The drive to my parent's home was a silent affair with the radio playing in the background. We took only one break and reached my parent's house in seven hours.

"Leave the bag in the car. Just in case things don't work out, we'll leave in an hour." I instructed Rishi.

He complied with a quick nod.

I rang the bell and then crossed my arms across my chest. I stood grounded for a bit, then did a quick twirl as if releasing the steam within me.

"I found parking in the shade," Rishi said with glee as he stood next to me while we waited for somebody to open the door. My smile to him felt forced even to myself.

Then he hugged me from the side. "All will be well. Just breathe, Dimple."

The month of June was making me sweat a lot. My cotton shirt already had stains of sweat. Thank God I had sprayed lots of perfume.

Just then, I heard my mom's voice near the door. She seemed to be talking to someone when she opened the door.

There was silence.

"Who is it?" I heard my dad inquire in a high decibel.

"It's 24DDD," she said with a grunt and then moved to the side, allowing me and Rishi to enter.

That sarcasm always made my heart beat as fast as a hummingbird's wings. Today was no different. Rishi chose to walk in while I stood grounded at the entrance.

"Aren't you coming inside," she asked.

Parents have such a love-hate relationship with their kids. They speak in a toxic way, but they'll still want them in their homes and feed them well.

"Mummy, I am 26 years old now, not 24 anymore." I tried to say with a broad, forced grin, hoping to ease the tension in the air.

"Time stood still for us the day you chose to elope, Dimple," she said with a straight face.

"Sure, mummy, and I have apologized over a hundred times for it. Can't you please forgive me?" I held her hands in mine and looked into her eyes with moist eyes. Within a minute, tears were flowing down both of us as if the director of this story had said 'action.'

"Can't I be your 26-year-old Dimple who was daring and determined?" I said in a somber tone, my tears continuing to flow.

"Determined since I was in love with Rishi, and so I dared to run away and get married, unlike other girls who would just choose to weep and create a drama like in Bollywood movies until their parents agree."

"I think we would have agreed too if you had chosen the drama over this daring event?" said my mom with a gingerly smile as we continued to hold each other's hands.

"But Mom, you and Papa never brought me up like that. You've always encouraged me to go for what my heart desired, so I opted for that route." I said with innocence.

While my mom was contemplating, I saw my daadi whose eyes were glassy as she stood near the sofa.

Just then, dad entered the scene. Seeing me and my mom's hands locked up, he nodded at Rishi and escorted him inside along with my daadi.

"Let the mother and daughter bring closure once and for all. You come and have tea with me." He said as he patted Rishi's back.

"That does not justify your taking such an action, Dimple. Do you know how our relatives scorned us over your senseless action? We had to avoid going out for months because of you. My kitty party friends made jokes about our family behind my back. I was their laughing stock for months," she said, this time with a scorned face, "And still am, sometimes," she muttered with a downward glance.

"I get it, mummy. I am very sorry. But you named me as deceitful and disrespectful, and it is affecting my relationship with Rishi. For the past two years, I've become an insecure, unstable person. I can't make a single decision since I feel I'll be reprimanded over it. I tend to lose my temper with him often. As a result, he avoids talking to me."

Now no parent can tolerate that!

Soon the tables changed, and she became defensive.

"Oh, my child." She was quick to hug me tight and cry, "I didn't know that my words would hurt you so much."

I enjoyed her touch and quickly stretched out my arms and locked my hands around her waist. It felt I had time traveled. Ever since I eloped with Rishi, I had lost that liberty. Today I got very emotional just doing this simple activity, which used to be an everyday event once.

The rosemary smell in her hair and my arms wrapped around her big wide waist was familiar yet felt so distant that I squeezed my eyes shut and pursed my lips to avoid bawling.

"Mummy, I am very sorry. Please forgive me." I said in a hushed tone, "I promise I'll not be so irrational again."

Mom let go of the hug and said with a jeer, "Honestly, I don't care if you make such a nonsensical decision since it'll be Rishi's problem."

I laughed and agreed.

We walked arm in arm toward the dining room, where all were seated.

"Mummy, how about I attend one of your kitty parties to show your friends how happily married I am? That will stop their backbiting."

"That's a wonderful idea." Mom tittered, and she clutched my arm tight.

My heart raced at that action, and I blushed hard. I felt like we were friends again.

Seeing us enter the room, my dad stood up, "So, is it a truce between the mother and daughter?" he inquired with a smile.

Mom nodded as she wiped her tears. "Yes, better to let it go since it's affecting her current life with Rishi."

Daadi was quick to spring in, "How come?"

"Daadi, he calls me fused bulb whenever I lose my temper over anything."

"Then why didn't you tell us earlier, beta?" inquired dad.

"Honestly, Papa, I didn't dare to open up until now. My past behavior would constantly chew on me whenever I visited you. Your expressions on how society was tormenting you were enough for me to be mute rather than say what was going wrong in my world...until I had a dream where my consciousness asked me to spring up before Rishi got another wife."

"Huh!"

"Another wife? Ha! No one else can compete to my Pearl. She is a gem," said my daadi as she hugged me fondly and kissed my forehead.

"But he is not to be blamed daadi, I would get irritated over the littlest of things. But now that you all have embraced my flaw, I'm sure I'll be the better wife."

Mom was quick to utter, "Flaws dear, not one flaw."

Dad gave out a peal of belly laughter, leaving me red-faced. But I was quick to justify, "I've promised him I'll be Dimple 2.0."

"Nah! I want the wife that I married. No new versions, please," said Rishi as he got up and patted my shoulders.

It seemed like an eternity I had sat with my parents and ate a meal accompanied by laughter, and the icing on the cake was Rishi by my side.

***

As the sun's hue started dimming from bright yellow to a deeper gold and started sinking below the horizon, I nudged Rishi to get our bag inside. It was such a surreal feeling to be sleeping in my room with my husband by my side.

"Listen, I plan on coming back next month and staying for a bit at my parent's place. I have some things to sort out."

"Whatever suits you, dear. So, what time should we leave tomorrow?" Rishi asked when we were by ourselves.

"Do we have to?"

"What do you mean? I have to go to work on Monday." Rishi said with wide eyes and a frown.

"I know," I whispered as I moved in closer with parted lips, and with a gentle stroke on his arm I said, "How about we take a detour before heading back home."

"What's on your mind?"

"How about we go back to Lucknow, revisit all those places from two years ago, and then drive home. Begin our life anew on a happier note."

"That'll be a full-day event. We don't have a change of clothes for tomorrow. You just packed our night suits," Rishi lamented.

"So what? We have our toothbrushes. We'll have squeaky clean teeth if not clean clothes." I said with a wide grin.

"Now that's the Dimple I married!" he said as he gently brushed my hair off my cheek and planted a kiss on it.

Please consider leaving a review of the book on Amazon and Goodreads. I'd appreciate it very much and it helps new readers find my stories.

Join me on Facebook

https://www.facebook.com/RuchiraKhanna01/

Follow me on Instagram

https://www.instagram.com/ruchira.khanna/

With Gratitude,

Ruchira

"Just be yourself," I said. "Relax!" A calm breeze fluttered my scarf and long shirt, caressing my skin as if to welcome me home.

Jay paced in front of the bench outside of the New Delhi International Airport. Exhaust fumes filled the air.

"Be cool." I watched a bank of clouds part to let the sun shine down on this city. "But, don't be frosty cool."

He glared at me.

"Be funny. But not that funny since you're not funny at all."

"Oh! Stop it, Meera!" Jay snapped, furiously blinking his eyes.

Despite Jay's mood, I couldn't contain my excitement. The leaves of the trees rustled like they were trying to whisper, *welcome back* in a code only I could decipher. I drummed my feet on the concrete and let childhood memories surface in my mind. Cars came and went, and I fixated on locating a specific car model and a particular driver.

Jay looked at his watch ten times. Finally, he asked, "When is Dada coming?"

I shrugged and kept watching.

"We could have spent our summer holidays at my parents' home, just as we celebrated Diwali. Your parents are never at home." He made a pout.

I stood up to face him, hands on my hips, "We had to come here to meet Dada and Tai. Dada needs to meet you and approve you with his eyes, Jay. You know the drill."

Jay winced. "Yes ... yes. I have heard how he has brought you up without saying a single word. I admire him, although don't you think it's too late for his approval?"

"Not really," I said, thinking back to when Dada came to know that I was on a dating spree instead of concentrating on getting my degree. "If he frowns at you as he did at Aditya in twelfth grade, I'll be dumping you." This time my voice was stern and sincere.

Jay snorted like a pig.

We had flown in from Dehradun where Jay and I are batch-mates at the engineering college. We met in my third year of college, and things were going so well that I traveled with him for Diwali holidays to his parents' house in Bangalore. As we completed one year of our courtship, I wanted him to come home and meet my side of the family—Tai and Dada. They are not my birth parents. They are much more than that. I wanted Dada's approval, the father figure who has never spoken a word to me! And yet, over the years, his eyes have schooled me, disciplined me from right and wrong, and urged me to understand the entire yin and yang that balances the world.

Dada's affection and my understanding were like twins that brought about my inner transformation.

A familiar honk interrupted my reveries. I squealed with delight like a schoolgirl and ran to the curb, waving at the driver who pulled up to park next to me. Dada. It had been four years since I last saw him.

I discreetly pinched Jay to remind him to be on his best behavior. He skewed his nose in return as if I had asked him to eat eggplant.

Dada got out of his car and walked toward me with agile steps. My eyes moistened when I noticed the gray hair in his mustache and sideburns.

Why didn't time stand still for me? I had a childish wish to be frozen by Queen Elsa's magical powers.

Dada's job was retained even after I left for college. He took on the responsibility of driving my biological parents around the town.

"Hello, Dada!" I greeted him with a hug.

Read more: viewbook.at/Throughhiseyes

The big, bold orange-colored star just like the oranges growing in sunny California was near the horizon ready to say goodbye for the day. The clouds in the sky were wearing a sepia tone as they held the sun firmly, even though the November winds were swaying them gently as if a baby's cradle was being rocked.

Life was bustling as usual in the small town of Santa Barbara in the southern region of California.

A car screeched its brakes and parked on the sidewalk after clicking off its turn signal. Sandra pushed open the driver-side door and was quick on her feet as she pulled open the massive entrance door to the daycare center.

Her stilettos were click-clacking as she pressed the lock button on her remote for the car. "I am sorry to be late again!" she said in a sincere tone as she approached the reception area. The lady sitting behind the counter looked bored and tired. She did not argue with Sandra. "Five dollars for being five minutes late," she declared as she scribbled something in her notebook.

"Mommy!" came a jubilant little boy's voice to which she was quick to go down on her knees and hug him tight.

After sharing a few kisses and smiles with Liam, she helped him with his jacket then dug into her wallet taking out a five-dollar bill and signed her son out. The mother-and-son duo walked out of the daycare center.

As she walked a few steps ahead of her son, her phone buzzed.

"Mom, I've invited my friend to come over on Saturday," said an excited Liam while dragging his rolling backpack with one hand and clumsily moving his feet to keep up with his Mom's steady steps while her attention was on the screen of her phone.

She was typing frantically on the phone with her long, brown hair falling over her shoulders. But as soon as she heard the words 'friend' and 'Saturday,' she paused quickly to turn around and ask in an ambivalent tone, "What? Could you repeat that?" she urged clicking to unlock her car with the remote making an audible noise, all the while giving her full attention to her son and tucking her hair behind her ear exposing her cream-colored complexion and sharp features.

"Yes, Mom, you heard it right. I'm having a friend over," he said as he climbed into the back seat of the car and buckled himself in his car seat.

With moist eyes and trembling hands, she was quick to kiss him on his forehead, "Wow! I'm excited about your playdate!"

She got into the driver's seat and was quick to place her shaky hands under her thighs and breathe in deeply and swiftly to compose herself. Sandra announced while looking at her son from the rearview mirror, "We have to celebrate! A playdate is happening after two months and three weeks! Jack O'Donald's tonight!"

"Yeah!" he shouted with joy creating dimples on his chubby cheeks, "I will have Dad's favorite."

Sandra looked at him as her heart skipped a beat.

******

While dipping her French fries in the ketchup, she paused and commented, "But we need to buy some toys. You hardly have any toys, Liam. What will you and your

"Mom!" a shout from Liam brought her out of her reverie, and she decided to start fixing dinner for the duo.
Read More: getbook.at/Ruch01

• 47 •

friend play with?"

Liam was sipping his chocolate shake and occasionally dipping his French fries into it. He was quick to respond, "I don't need any toys. I have my dog."

Sandra was aghast over the comment, and she merely froze with her eyes wide open forgetting to chew.

Sweat was quick to develop on her forehead, and Liam was smart to realize why. "I meant I was lucky to have Yogi and no toys."

Sandra forced a smile and nodded affirmatively. "Exactly! Now that Yogi is no more…" She paused for a bit and tried to swallow, which took forever to do, and continued, "We should have toys. Although, I am always curious about what you do in your room behind closed doors. I only see a toy truck and a couple of Jedi masks that are always dirty along with your soiled clothes and the wet floor."

"But I just want to do that!" Liam raised his voice to assert his point.

Sandra gave him an unfriendly frown while rolling her eyes indicating they are in public, and he calmed down.

Soon, they were driving home with a chirpy Liam in the back seat while Sandra's head was tilted to one side. She was wearing a frown on her face while occasionally massaging the front of her neck as if smoothing the skin that seemed to have become wrinkled in a matter of two months.

Sandra opened the door to a cold house that gave Liam and her the shivers courtesy of the month of November. But in a matter of a few minutes, a warm draft started to blow from the vents even before she had time to adjust the thermostat to a sixty-eight-degree- Fahrenheit temperature. That action always puzzled her, but the fact that it left her and Liam warm and cozy gave her no need to investigate further.

Liam's homework was the usual addition and subtraction mathematics, but this time it was a tad bit more interesting since the teacher had introduced the concept of money. Making sentences from words was also not a challenge for Liam since he was comfortable with them thanks to the author, Enid Blyton, and his stay-at-home dad who would read to him all cuddled up with Yogi in his favorite blanket. He finished his homework in no time and announced his playtime, shutting his bedroom door while Sandra went back to her work.

She drew out a long breath at first since she was still adjusting to him getting his homework done so fast. Third grade was proving to be a home run thanks to Sam who had laid a solid academic foundation as did his school teacher.

She then slouched over her laptop continuing to try to decipher the code to debug a particular application she was testing for a company. Her shoulders and neck had tightened. Deadlines at work always made her nervous, but she dared not complain since she wanted to keep her mind occupied, or else she feared the loneliness and the guilt she carried would wear her down.

Just then, a cool breeze blew in out of nowhere, and it threw her back on the chair. She closed her eyes as her tense shoulders seemed to gradually relax. She reminisced about how Sam, her deceased husband, would pamper her with a massage whenever she was under pressure. This unknowingly brought a smile to her lips while she relaxed her shoulders as her neck arched in a certain way.